THE MOUNTAIN
A meditation on the consequences of an obsession

J.S. Lan

CW00857715

Introductic

Two and a half miles from Rhayader, in Wales, is a 1,558 foot hill called Gamallt. It can also be thought of as a mountain. Using the author's encounter with Gamallt, this story, written in the form of a meditation, explores some of the ways in which philosophical and scientific ideas about perception and reality have led to thought-provoking ideas about what can be said to be real. It also seeks to loosen the apparent incompatibility of fantasy and the logical preoccupations of philosophers and scientists. It uses, in part, the parallels between "to exist is to be perceived" and the suggestion, often found in writers dealing with quantum mechanics, that human consciousness is somehow involved in descriptions of what, at least in the sub-atomic world, occurs when observations are made. The assumption that there is an objective world independent of any observers, and the possible rejection of such a view, might be said to find expression in both philosophy and science. The mountain becomes a backdrop for the suggestion that both disciplines, for all their justifiable preoccupation with logic, can also be embraced by way of imagination.

dedicated to members of the philosophy department of Lancaster University, 1968-1975

Of the three hundred and eighty-two kilograms of moon rock lifted with surprising ease – gravity on the moon being less than two tenths that on the surface of the Earth – and brought back to our planet by the astronauts who participated in the six moon landings which occurred between 1969 and 1972, most has remained in the hands of scientific institutions and public laboratories. Only a tiny fraction has disappeared into the hands of private individuals, greedy or otherwise obsessive collectors who, no doubt having paid substantial sums of money for their acquisitions, are forced to keep them in isolation from all of the other rocks on the earth, even the oldest ones. These, if modern science is to be believed, once formed part of the primeval body which suffered a spectacular collision with some large, asteroid-like object some 4.6 billion years ago, ejecting a plume of vaporised matter which, trapped in the ecliptic, eventually coalesced to form the moon, orbiting us to this day in the same plane as the one in which we circle the sun but leaving our planet tipped, by the impact, enough to secure the seemingly eternal song and dance of the seasons. So it is that gravity, elsewhere such an impersonal force throughout the universe, seems, by way of the tides that make the seas seem disobedient of the general stillness of the earth, expressive of a longing for some brutal but sentimental reunion. Things, however, being what they so often are – the opposite of what they seem – the moon is in fact slowly spiralling away from us at a rate of about 4 cm per year. All is not lost, however; for it so happens that, at some time in the very distant future, the friction between the tidally tormented oceans and the Earth's surface will have slowed down our rotation (a phenomenon that was, remarkably, predicted long ago by the philosopher Immanuel Kant) so much that a solar day will equal a lunar month, and the shy retreat of the moon will come to an end. Our planet will then present the same side to its satellite, just as we now only ever see one side of the moon. Like lovers unable to take their eyes off each other, Moon and Earth will be locked in a gravitational impasse; a situation called, I believe, by astronomers a stable configuration. No moon rock, when all is said and done, will ever cease, one way or another, to keep us company, and the astronauts' samples will never be too far from their first or their second home. But of the incalculably larger tonnage of marbles that have passed through the hands of children from, at the very least, Roman times until the day I played my first game in one of the streets that set the course of my childhood, only one has ever stayed with me, and then only in my mind. I played a game and won, but the boy whose fabulous red and white ally I had knocked into a hole and which should therefore have been mine, refused to hand it over. I claimed my prize; and rather than let me have it, he threw it into the stream on whose dusty bank we were playing. I won and lost a good many marbles over the next few summers, but never encountered one that quite matched the beauty that I had coveted. I lost interest in them as I grew up, but part of me still wants the one that I never held in my hand. Many years later, the curving streaks of colour that were embedded in its pure white form were to seem to me to be identical to the rounded thoracic segments of a rolled-up trilobite; and indeed Richard Fortey, in his obsessive, passionate and lucidly written book *Trilobite!* has likened an enrolled trilobite to a marble, so perfect is its rotundity. The story I am about to tell, of my recent activities, is, I was forced to admit to myself some time ago, nothing more than an account of my struggle, which has sometimes unnerved me but more often filled me with a deep satisfaction, to retrieve what has belonged to me for such a long time but which has never been in my possession. It is a task which has loosened my convictions regarding the occasionally brutal differences between the world we can touch and the world of the mind, and which I see now as an attempt to unroll something which has long occupied both.

I have placed the latest addition to my collection in the space which I prepared for it. My wife does not yet know what I did to make room for the beautiful stone which caught my eye when we were walking along the grassy banks of the River Wye, during the last, melancholy day of our holiday. It was just a stone among others, half of it dark brown under the water, the other half bleached by the sun; but a passing cloud brought it to life, and when I saw the ridges and hollows formed by who knows how many years of sucking and splashing, all that love and indifference afforded by the river – then I knew instantly that I had to have it. I sat and looked at it for a whole afternoon. The whitened part that was jutting out of the river was dead, like a cleansed and sanitised fossil; but the dark shape under the water – that was something else, as much a part of the living river as I was whenever I waded in it, except for that last day in Wales. Is it ever possible to enjoy the last day of a perfect holiday? The journey back to the scene you needed to get away from starts nudging at your elbows, like a driving instructor: hold the wheel so, release it with the left hand to change gear so, expect heavy traffic at the approach to the motorway...my last days are always like that; I wander around fields or trudge up a mountain path with my hands at my side, but I'm already steering my car back to our drive. That's how it was that afternoon: I kept staring at the dry part of the stone, thinking, I'm still immersed in my holiday but dry thoughts are entering my head, bleaching the day. Everything was turning white. But I snapped out of these desiccated reveries and jumped down from the river bank so that I could touch the stone. The dry part was hot from the afternoon sun, but the submerged surfaces were cold and slippery. It was bigger than I had thought. It is best to think of river rocks as icebergs: the bit you can see does not

3

tell you what you need to know if you have designs on it. It moved when I pulled at it, sending clouds of disturbed sediment downstream, and after I rolled it over I had to use a piece of driftwood to clean off some kind of slimy material which looked as if it had been there a long time. Then I washed it, fondling the crevices and smooth concavities as the river surged over it. I was going to say that I placed it in a sunny spot to dry when it was free of all trace of the river, but that would be careless; the river had made it, its very shape was the result of water and sand and pebbles, and probably some larger rocks, sculpting it from whatever form it had had when, long ago, it had first encountered the abrasive ministrations of the eddies and torrents that shaped and reshaped the riverbed onto which it had fallen. Maybe there were no smooth faces or gentle curves for a long time; only rough irregularities and sharp edges arguing with the flow of the water season after season until, at last, the battle was lost. Newly broken stones are aggressive, are they not, until one or more of the so-called elements have worn them down into the contours of submission? This idea was at the back of my mind as I sat looking at my stone, trying to imagine what it had looked like when it first broke free of whatever chunk of the earth's crust it had been a part of. Perhaps it had even had one perfectly flat surface, a segment of one of those impossibly straight strata that confuse our dogmatic assumptions about the artificial and the organic. But whatever it looked like, it was destined to change the moment it joined the river, from the moment the first atom was ripped from it. Rocks are not the everlasting things we casually take them to be, after all: they were something else before and will be something else again in due course. Marine mud becomes slate; sandstone cathedrals erode in the wind and will one day turn back into grains of sand. Ideas last longer than rocks, I thought, as I sat by my stone at the water's edge and allowed exuberant thoughts to get the better of me. But then the sun went in, and a light shower of rain prompted me to manoeuvre my new

4

possession into my rucksack. When I got back to our base I heaved it into the boot of our car and covered it with an old waterproof anorak. After several glasses of wine I had forgotten how heavy it was. But even alongside Isobel and among friends, I started navigating my way home again: the holiday was truly over.

My latest stone is once more one among many, larger than all of those I collected previously but not at all out of place. I have laid it to rest alongside a large-leaved Hosta sieboldiana; in front of it are numerous limestone slabs and chunks of granite, with an eye-catching and very irregular piece of quartz placed for maximum effect on a bed of Thymus serpyllum. But it is the holiday stone which demands the longest scrutiny. I am hoping that Isobel will not notice that I dug up a rather weary-looking specimen of Dierama pulcherrima – Angel's fishing rod – which has rarely flowered and may well be in the wrong kind of soil – to provide a suitable space for the fugitive from the river. Sitting now in the shade afforded by an unpruned wisteria, I can begin planning our next holiday, and perhaps choose a provisional site for the next arrival. I am not a quarryman, but I like to feel that I have a modest role in the great human enterprise of shifting soil and rock – I should say re-arranging it - from one part of the planet to another. If you take away all the other things – the wars, the marriages, the pieces of paper and the things that get written on them – our real legacy is the ground we walk on. Nothing in what we choose to call history can possibly compare, in significance, to such real events as the Caledonian Orogeny: the mountain building episode whose last convulsions took place some 400 million years ago toward the end of the Silurian period. A great crustal contraction; the folding of sediments, the intrusion of granites, a long upward thrust with huge consequences: vast mountain chains, the deformation of the Lake District, the shrinking of the distance between Northern Scotland and South Wales and even – not so far from where I found my latest stone – the transformation of mud into the slate belt around Llanberis. And those long, slow, so often marine geological crescendos echo in our own small endeavours: consider the Jurassic origins of the lithographic stone of Solnhofen; the graphite in the Skiddaw slate deposits near Keswick, laid to rest until it was born again in millions of restless pencils; or the endless upheavals that were necessary for the production of chalk, with infinitely small pieces of which a succession of teachers tried, with the help, I like to think, of blackboards made of Welsh slate, to put a bit of sense into me when I was a boy. But where was I? Thinking about the next holiday, I seem to remember. It will be back to the Wye. I want to obtain an even bigger stone, one that will establish a truly intimate connection between our house, where we dream of holidays, and the immense rock which oversees all of my adventures on the banks of the river: Gamallt, the scree laden and heather festooned eminence in whose shade we all played at being truly free, and from behind which, one early evening last summer, Mars appeared in the form of a beacon in the night sky, brighter than Sirius and more orange than Betelgeuse, at the moment of its closest encounter with Earth. This decision is going to present me with some difficulties; heaving the last one into the car boot, after carting it up from the river valley, was hard work that took me near to the limit of my strength. What concerns me even more is the struggle I am having to set a limit on my aspirations; each time I picture the bend in the river where, each summer, I find most of my trophies, I seem to set eyes on an ever larger rock; one whose visible part, let alone the submerged mass on which it sits, is far too big for me to dislodge and certainly not a candidate for transportation. I am starting to entertain thoughts about rocks that are big enough for me to sit on, or which might require me to leave most of our luggage behind and drive back here with the boot half open to accommodate them. I have begun to wonder if I could go online and purchase, maybe from eBay, a trailer sturdy enough to support something that really deserves to be called a rock. Conveying dramatically heavy chunks of the landscape from place to place is not an impossible task; Stonehenge, after all, was not constructed from anything that lay immediately to hand on Salisbury Plain.. Those eighty bluestone slabs were dragged all of 200 miles from the Prescelly Hills in Pembrokeshire and assembled onsite. I like to think that those who completed the task were convinced that the moon, when it passed overhead and repeated its conjunctions with the circles of stones, did so because they had helped it. So with the help of a plan and a car, what is to stop me bringing a hefty piece of Silurian mudstone from Gamallt to Cumbria?

There: my difficulties are mounting. I began by acknowledging that my project is threatening to become over-ambitious; but no sooner have I admitted that I may be over-reaching myself, than I go even further. I've started to picture myself draping ropes as thick as my wrists over some moss-covered boulder, shouting instructions to a bemused farmer on a tractor. I think I need to bring myself to heel. It is time for me to do what I have so often done since I was a student, and remind myself of the rather unrealistic ideas of Bishop Berkeley. It was in 1685 that some heroic woman whose name is unknown to me gave birth – that most physical of human experiences – to the boy subsequently known to the world as George Berkeley, who, before he died in 1753, embarked on a philosophical adventure that led him to insist that there is no such thing as physical reality, only the mental reality that he (you have to put yourself in his place here) perceived. Subsequent generations of philosophers either subscribed enthusiastically to his solipsism, presumably taking care never to speak to each other, though capable I assume of becoming fearless boxers;- or rejected it, insisting, as did for instance Immanuel Kant, that in order to be properly conscious at all we need to assume the existence of a physical world inhabited by things and people whose otherness, and occupancy of different parts of the same space as the one we were swanning around in, was distinguishable from such subjective impostors as dreams or hallucinations. But of course the most notorious rejection of all was recounted by James Boswell, who reported that Samuel Johnson, the good doctor who gave us the dictionary, dismissed Berkeley's theory by kicking a large stone and declaring, "I refute it thus." Berkeley had died, as I have said, in 1753, which was just as well, because I have often thought how satisfying it would have been for Dr Johnson to have encountered Bishop Berkeley and to have thumped him, very hard, on the head with a copy of his very substantial dictionary, so as to then be able to say, "Just take me through the argument again, George." Anyway, the rocks I keep thinking about are a lot bigger than the one Dr Johnson kicked, and I must try to remember that when I begin to fantasize, as I did a moment ago, about finding a truly massive but solipsistically malleable one, one which I could fashion into something like a round shape and roll, as if it were a ball, all the way from the river to our garden, then I am being unrealistic, even if I imagine leaving a trail of damaged cars and road signs so as to acknowledge the plastic nature of my dream.

Esse est percipi: of course it is an inadequate philosophical position. How could Michael Collins, the first man ever to be truly alone, have survived if he had subscribed to Berkeley's ideas? As the Command Service Module entered that part of its moon orbit that took it into the realm of the lunar far side, the earth disappeared to modern science and not just from his solitary vision. Nothing to see, and no radio contact either. *To exist is to be perceived* was not going to sustain him in his isolation – even the moon itself no more than a round black void, a circle in which there were no stars - until he sailed round the edge and back into the world that Galileo and the inquisition argued about. Nor would the oversimplification, resembling a faulty translation from the Latin, of *to exist is to perceive* have afforded him any comfort. I like to credit him with the first unambiguously therapeutic application of Descartes' seemingly more modest proposition: *I think, therefore I am.* And I choose to believe, because it gratifies me so to do, that he was instrumental in naming the hilly region of the moon called Descartes' Highlands. But down below on the surface of the Sea of Tranquility, Buzz Aldrin, I like also to think, was walking in Dr Johnson's territory. What did he refute when he left his footprint in the lunar dust – churned over, we are told, by the constant rain of micrometeorites every 12 million years and covering rocks that are 4½ billion years old? Would he have felt the need to refute anything in the face of a landscape that so clearly existed but had never before been perceived by anyone?

The winter days are dragging on; the Hosta alongside the stone was cut down by frost some time ago, and the kitchen window has for several evenings been visited by the fluttering investigative patter of the November moth, known to me since I was a boy as *Oporinia dilutata*. Without the Hosta's softening foliage my biggest fear has been realized: all of my stones, even the one that has pride of place, look unimposing, even lost, in the denuded spaces of the garden. It is hard for me to cope with the further modification of my arrangements for the next holiday which this diminution of the rockery, as I like to call it, has unleashed. Something dramatic has happened. There has been an escalation, an exciting but crazy development in what I intend to do. It started when I was endeavouring to be fair to Bishop Berkeley, trying to give his abandonment of the material world one more hearing in the light of modern science. Was Dr Johnson aware, when he kicked the rock, that his very act of refutation would have released some of the atoms whose assembled presence, in large numbers, we choose to call matter? I remembered what I had imagined about my river rock, lighter, by a few molecules, as soon as it was set upon by the water and abrasive particles of the river into which it had fallen, or perhaps found itself as a result of the languid violence of glacial meltwaters. In geological time, had he lived that long, the great man could have repeatedly kicked the rock until it was barely substantial enough to register its presence, let alone be able to furnish a sensory experience vivid enough to justify the empirical retort for which he is, among of course other things, remembered. It is, indeed, fortunate that down-to-earth philosophers of his sort enjoy, at best, the brief opportunity for reflection that we call longevity, which offers only the most fleeting encounter with the stuff and bric-a-brac of the universe. Empiricism, after all, only works if you are unable to linger long enough to witness the continuing metamorphosis, or indeed disappearance, of whatever you stumble across during your time as a sentient being. Real venerability, on a cosmic scale, could probably only sit comfortably alongside the kind of reality proposed by Arthur Schopenhauer, who found himself unable to refute Kant's arguments and gave us his version in *The World as Will and Idea*, whereby what most of us would call reality is merely a palimpsest arising from our spiritual and sensory encounters with a fundamentally unknowable bedrock. I make the world as I know it, he said, and I can acknowledge that the world changes because I do not. What permanence can I ascribe, then, to the collectables with which I have constructed my rockery? I can't be bothering with pebbles any more, nor even with what I used to call substantial boulders. I need to concern myself with something big enough to outlast my dreams, yet also, insofar as it looms before me as something real, made substantial by them. My thoughts have turned to Gamallt.

Could I steal a piece of mountain? I may have to postpone, perhaps forever, the decision I made to buy a new car and have also, without telling Isobel, placed in jeopardy our ability to make further visits to Wales after the one to which I am now looking forward with increased and fervent excitement. I have arranged to hire a lorry and with it a powerful pneumatic drill together with some lifting equipment which will be operated from the cab. Just now, after several glasses of wine, I revealed my ideas to her. We will travel to Wales in the lorry, I told her, our suitcases and other luggage covered by a tarpaulin sheet; and I shall spend the week cutting a massive slab of rock from the side of Gamallt. I cannot say I got the response which I was hoping for. Isobel responded very negatively, raising a string of objections – the immensity of my project, the disruption to our holiday, the certainty that I would face prosecution for damaging, not to mention removing, a section of the Powys countryside – and finally stating, with an air of finality which I am unlikely to be able to counter, that she would not, either under the circumstances I proposed nor any others which I might dream up, consent to travelling to Wales in a lorry. My scheme, then, at least as I have envisaged it over the last few days, will have to be modified – I will not say abandoned, although it will of course be necessary for me to cancel the bookings for the lorry and for the cutting and lifting gear. I don't have much room for manoeuvre; I tried proposing the use of our car with a trailer, even though this would involve a compromise regarding the possible dimensions of my rock, but Isobel would have none of it. Perhaps after a good night's sleep a better course of action will present itself to me. To that end, I intend to reflect, as I lie in bed and wait for the light to fade, on the Taoist principle which I came across in my earlier years but have not until now considered worth thinking about: *better to have too little than to have too much.*

It is too silly to even joke about. Just now, as my wife was booking our next – I believe it will be our seventh – escape to the longhouse in which we will all assemble, each of us first turning to face the mountain in order to renew our spiritual vigour and also to re-establish the feeling, with which we are all familiar, that we have been absent from its grandeur for only the briefest interlude – I remembered the feeling about

Gamallt with which I am always assailed when I turn, my homage paid to it, to enter the building: the conviction that it is by the tiniest of margins a little closer to the doorway than it was the previous year. No sooner that memory, than I was beset with the most ridiculous thoughts: I started imagining the monumental task of shifting the mountain, even if by the smallest, barely perceptible amount, toward our house in Cumbria, so that they, too could be a little closer together. I believe that I was led into this embarrassingly futile reverie by way of what I suspect is my imperfect understanding of some of the laws of physics, in particular the one given to us by Newton which states that *action and reaction are equal and opposite*. If that is the case, I was thinking, then if I lean on a mountain, it cannot push against my hand any harder than I can push against its slope. It's not the unequal contest I would, without reflection, take it to be. When my wife put the phone down and announced that the booking was done and dusted, or in the bag or anyway some such expression of accomplishment, I found myself in the grip of a most riveting feeling of optimism: a conviction, which I was quite unable to question or subject to any kind of intellectual caution, that I would be able to formulate a plan whereby *the distance between the landscape of our holidays, and our home, would be lessened.*

The huge wooden door is open and everyone is outside save me. We all arrived during the afternoon, so the usual excursion to the river is under way before the sun goes down, but without me. I volunteered to prepare the kitchen for tonight's meal because I wanted to clarify my ideas, which I have not yet revealed to anyone other than Isobel. As is usual with me one set of thoughts has regressed to another, and I am preoccupied with Bishop Berkeley again, or rather, to be more precise, with Dr Johnson's foot. Of the countless discussions of his conversation with Boswell, the one which has most recently exercised me is that by David Deutsch in his rather difficult book *The Fabric of Reality*. Deutsch is at pains to emphasise that Dr Johnson was in effect proposing a criterion for reality identical to the one used, he stresses, in science, namely, that *if something can kick back, it exists.* The doctor was aware that he decided to kick the rock, but had no part in the state of affairs which immediately followed his action, which was that he felt the rebound. The rock did not exist because he perceived it; it existed independently, just as Isaac Newton, to whose theories Berkeley's metaphysical claims were, in part, a riposte, had memorably asserted when he assumed the existence of matter, occupying space and, in its many forms, participating in the great games of cause and effect whose laws he had presented to the world in 1687. It was surely Newton that the Bishop had in mind when he wrote, with the kind of ingenuous modesty with which philosophers unveil their most radical and far-reaching claims, "I must not say the words thing, substance etc. have been the cause of mistakes. But the not reflecting on their meaning. I will still be for retaining the words. I only desire that men would think before they speak and settle the meaning of their words." How uncomfortable Berkeley would have been if he had travelled, as a passenger, in one of the Apollo spacecraft, Apollo 8, let us say, and had heard, as it coasted, after a particularly forceful manifestation of action and reaction, toward the moon with its rocket motor subsequently silent, the comment sent back to Mission Control by astronaut Bill Anders: "Isaac Newton is doing most of the driving right now." Having said that, I am pretty uncomfortable myself, because I cannot rid myself of the worry that in order to proceed with any confidence, I need Berkeley as much as I need Newton and Dr Johnson. When I toy with the deeply satisfying idea that I could push against the mountain with some measure of success, however infinitesimally small, I suspect that it is necessary for me to assume, as did Samuel Johnson, that rock is real. But all of the machinations – the mental ropes and pulleys – which are crystalising in my mind, and which require a major effort on my part to sustain themselves as sensible – all of this is really an act of imagination. I have to visualise both Gamallt and our house, located as it is a couple of hundred miles away in Cumbria, and then hold, in my head, the notion of simultaneous action being exerted on each of them (which will, I hope, involve my wife, as I shall explain later). This is the Bishop's territory – I couldn't ever, in reality, see both places at once, and there is no God that I believe in, forever rescuing Berkeley's world by perceiving it regardless of the fortuitous presence or absence of humans. So now I'm recalling Berkeley's most fundamental assertion: " 'Tis on the nature and meaning and import of Existence that I chiefly insist." And, regressing as I usually do, I now call to mind his admonitory declaration: "The Vast, Widespread, Universal Cause of our Mistakes is that we do not consider our own notions, I mean consider them in themselves, fix, settle and determine them."

Which makes the mountain easiest to shift: approaching it as something I perceive, and therefore in part subject to movements of my mind? or as a thing, a lump of matter trapped in the laws of nature and thus open to communication and re-arrangement of a more physical kind? If Schopenhauer were available, by some shift of time, for a few moments of metaphysical banter, I would invite him to consider the fact that I am caught, right now, between a rock and a hard place. And I'm not alone in this logical arena. Ever since Heisenberg proclaimed that it is impossible to measure both the position and the momentum of a nuclear particle – indeed the more accurately you measure one, the more imprecise becomes the ascertainable value of the other, the world of physics has debated the worrisome implication which he blandly announced: that there is no point in considering to be part of reality that which cannot, by any conceivable experiment, be observed. Unswerving supporters tell us that this points to a fundamental property of quantum systems, and not, as the more down-to-earth citizen might assume, a statement about the inadequacy of even the latest measuring apparatus; and that an electron, say, *does not have* a position or a momentum until an act of measurement takes place. Einstein famously retorted that this is tantamount to saying that the moon does not exist unless someone is looking at it. That may well be the case, has been a common retort from the quantum community: there are many properties of "things" in the sub-atomic world which only seem to spring into existence when we, as conscious observers, scrutinise or measure them in some way, and all big things are after all made entirely of the sometimes ghostly bits and pieces that are subject to the hugely verified laws of quantum mechanics. How extraordinary it is that after so many years, during which the world of science has ever more confidently presented its *Weltanschauung* as the ultimate paradigm of objectivity, there should be an increasingly confident message, delivered from centres of learning to those of us who languish in the backwaters of common sense, to the effect that reality is in some profound way a momentary product of consciousness. Berkeley would have been over the moon…

We walked down to the river this morning and arranged ourselves along the bank as if to recline in the shade. But Isobel found a perfectly round pebble and threw it into the water. It was a Pavlovian situation; everyone else immediately began rummaging among the shingle for flat stones to skim downstream. This is a sport at which every one of us is convinced he can excel. You pick up a smooth pebble, preferably not irregular and as thin as possible without being light enough to render it ineffectual. You curl your index finger around part of the circumference and grip it with your thumb and the other three fingers, holding it horizontally. Then you hurl it as hard as you can, always in the belief that it will ricochet off the surface of the water like a bouncing bomb heading for a dam. Your pebble never travels as far as those flung by one other competitor. Isobel suggested that we try to clear a line of white rocks traversing the river about thirty feet away, so we all set to it. The competition to achieve it first was won by Woody, ever the perfectionist, who judged perfectly the compromise needed between hitting the water close enough to the rocks to clear them in one bounce and ensuring that the point of contact allowed the missile time to rise enough to avoid smashing into them. His winning throw was achieved with a pale grey, perfectly dry oval slate, which he licked on what was to be its underside. He informed us, with a grin, that this would lubricate its encounter with the water, avoiding the split-second delay that would occur if it had first to soak up moisture into its porous surface. He had also, I noticed, placed the winning stone in his armpit for a few moments, I guess to warm it in keeping with some theory or other about airborne motion. Such attention to detail! I got nowhere, partly, I have to say, because I began selecting ever heavier stones to throw, sacrificing my chances of success for the vulgar satisfaction of causing larger and larger splashes – the momentary triumph of stone over water. Then the sun came out and the prospect of swimming brought the competition to a close. I had wandered some distance downstream in my quest for heavy stones, and as I listened to the splashes and shouts of those from whom I had retreated, I found myself thinking of them as belonging to the river, so much so that their merriment seemed to be emanating not from them but from the water itself. It brought into my mind a snatch of verse written by Christopher Marlowe:...*by shallow rivers, to whose falls/melodious birds sing madrigals*. Later that afternoon, when I had once again separated from my companions, I glimpsed, through the trees on the far bank, two young women walking along the road that ran past Gamallt and parallel to the river. They were singing, and it was madrigals once more. I knew why Marlowe's lines had come back to me. Piscator, one of the characters in Isaac Walton's treatise on angling, heard two milkmaids singing Marlowe's poem *The Shepherd's Plea* and the response to it, *The Nymph's Reply*, written by Sir Walter Ralegh; he persuaded them to perform once more for him and his fellow angler by offering them one of the fish he had caught that day. I had no fish, and only a pebble in my hand and a rock on my mind, so the girls did not repeat their song for me. But their bright clothing flashed intermittently in the spaces between the trees until they finally vanished from sight.

After the skimming, I began to walk downstream. I made my way past the wetlands, where countless dragonflies repeatedly showed their unconscious mastery of the air in interlocking parabolas of shimmering flight over the dark green spike rush that covered the ground between the ponds. Picking up a handful of tiny pebbles, I began throwing them, one at a time, into the air. It is sometimes possible to divert the flight of a hawking dragonfly by doing this; for a very brief moment, it may swerve, if you are lucky, toward the projectile until it realises that it is not an insect. The same thing is possible with bats: slightly larger pebbles may be mistaken for moths, although like dragonflies they veer away at the last moment and you have to be careful, in the dark, that what you have thrown into the air does not compensate the bats by falling on your head. On this occasion, the dragonflies did not respond, so I discarded the remaining pebbles. They were probably too large in comparison with whatever prey was on the wing. And the bats had reminded me of something I had read about Rhayader church, where there had been a tradition, in the 9th century, for mourners to throw a stone onto a spot near the church wall saying 'Cam ar dy ben' – a stone upon thy head. I decided to be more careful, and watched the dragonflies without intervening.

Few people, when they glimpse these creatures celebrating their position at the top of their food chain, realise the long unwitnessed preparation which they have undergone, or should I say enjoyed, just above the mud among the tangled fronds and branching mazes of pondweed where their prey multiply as if for their benefit. Some of the larger species spend as long as five years underwater as nymphs, a label that does not, with its overtones of the distractions of Greek mythological adventures or Debussy–serenaded relaxation among dreamy foliage, offer any indication of the savage and terrifying efficiency of their ability to kill and consume what they hunt. They need only to approach some hapless juvenile at the bottom of the pond – a tadpole, or a small fish still coming to terms with the operation of its swim bladder in order to stay deeply submerged during the cold water of the winter – to within a distance that would be, in human terms, about six feet – and remain motionless, as if meaning no harm; then they release, in some kind of explosive burst of muscular tissue, an extendible jaw which fastens itself, like two inward curving javelins striking home with perfect co-ordination, into the soft and immediately doomed tissue of the fellow changeling whose vital juices they then immediately begin to extract. In this way, the DNA of countless small creatures wriggling and swimming in still water is appropriated and re-organised into the mysterious instructions that will cause the nymphs to climb, one summer day, the stem of a convenient reed so as to emerge into the sunlight, where they remain as still as a stone until their penultimate armour of chitin splits to reveal a new self adorned with miraculously delicate but fiendishly powerful wings, re-enforced with a mosaic-like network of hardened veins; wings so strong that they can stop in mid air and fly backwards if the pursuit of their own prey – they feed of course on other insects – demands it. At the moment of their emergence, they are pale and relatively colourless; but after a few days have elapsed they take on the emerald greens, the sapphire blues, the sunflower yellows and the blood reds of their final livery, and commence, the moment their splendid body paints are dried, to hunt and kill those insects which are smaller and slower on the wing than themselves. Their successes remind me of the way in which raptors of every conceivable variety have usurped the logic of Berkeley's principle and turned it on its head: for so often, in the world of the hunter and the hunted, *to be perceived, is to cease to exist.* As I drew near the fallen tree which marked the end of the last wetland enclosure, I found myself reciting another passage from Isaac Walton, whose *Compleat Angler* I had taken home from the local library which was my second home when I was a boy: "I will walk the meadows, by some gliding stream, and there contemplate the lilies that take no care and those very many other various little living creatures that are not only created, but fed, man knows not how, by the goodness of the God of Nature." After I had read that closing passage from the book, whose earlier pages had convinced me that I must become a fisherman long before I left school, I had often wondered how I might live as if I myself were a lily, with nothing to do but dream in the sun, until the ceaseless flow of my own years revealed to me the predatory dominance of time, the intangible guest bringing the food for every feast that is ever enjoyed. We are drinking Chablis tonight. I brought along two bottles of *Montmains* and *Mont de Milieu*, which I selected from my cellar partly because they are delicious and partly, I have to admit, as a result of the resonance the vineyard names have for me these days. It is a happy accident that the vineyards of Nierstein, whose wines I drink as frequently as I can, often include the German word for a mountain: Oelberg, Rosenberg, Bruderberg, Kranzberg, Paterberg, Bergkirche;- although I have to say that some of those sites look more like hills, and hills of fairly modest proportions at that. But if clusters of words begin to attach themselves to the peccadillos and passions of our lives, I'm all for helping them along. Hugh Johnson, I told those who were listening, once memorably described the stony, minerally taste of great Chablis as like sucking a pebble. I am particularly drawn to this idea, for it implies that something can be both wet and dry in so definite and uncompromising a way that it offers me a transition from the dogmas of Aristotelian logic, which obsessed me when I was young, to the dreamier suggestions of the Eastern mystics, whose writings have led me to half-believe that all paths, no matter how straight they seem, are forked. And what if each fork is itself divided? It is with such a dream that contemporary physicists try to remove the paradox and mystery from quantum mechanics: the dream of many worlds, whereby reality is exfoliated into a multiverse. Two such parallel universes speak eloquently to me; one vindicating, and therefore bringing closure, to Newton's opinion, expressed in a letter to a Cambridge scholar, that if the universe was finite, everything would eventually be drawn, by gravitation, together to form one spherical lump of matter – a universe where no shift of position would be necessary or indeed make any sense; and an infinite one in which I was a grasshopper and Gamallt, a molehill – bestowing upon me the freedom to sit on its summit and make stridulatory music all summer long. There is of course a second idea which has taken hold of the more imaginative of the cosmologists who seek to compile a catalogue, and a description, of everything that exists; one which, while it does not multiply entities as dramatically as the concept of a multiverse, nevertheless seeks to effect a similarly dramatic change to our notion of their nature. It is an idea which reminds me of a conversation which I had with Plume, when we were animated with the passions of youth and carried all of our discussions to the extremes of their logical implications. I had drawn his attention to the striking similarities between the then prevailing picture of the structure of the atom, with its nucleus and its orbiting attendant particles, and the larger architecture of the cosmos, with its suns and planets and galactic Catherine wheels; and I went on to suggest that we, along with everything else that occupied the observable universe, might simply be the particulate contents of a glass of wine which was, even as we spoke, being raised to someone's lips; and that the universe might actually consist of an infinite series of such collections of matter and energy, both smaller and larger than we could imagine. He found my vision of an extended universe too prosaic, leaving, as it did, the nature of things unaltered; and he proposed instead that we consider the universe to be a poem, which some form of intelligent life, somewhere, was in the course of reciting. Now, all these years later, it has been mooted that everything – all of us and the universe that we inhabit – may be nothing more than a computer simulation, the playful product of a machine with unlimited memory that is able to create a virtual reality equal, in scope and complexity, to the one we take for granted. That such a reality would be interactive appears to satisfy those who envisage it that we, who have the gift of perception and of thought, are not what we think we are; we are independent agents only insofar as we have been programmed to be. The phenomenon of consciousness, which no physicist has ever been able to convert, in a reductive explanation, to the stuff that obeys the laws of physics, is thus cast aside and left where some of them have always wanted it to be: in a cloud of illusory non-being, a bogus category lacking independent existence and properly seen only as an emergent phenomenon, one that cannot grasp its origin in the inanimate world. In a similar fashion, and with comparable arrogance, are we told, quite often, that since the brain is a necessary condition for the mind, then the latter is no more than an untidy and complicated behavioural spasm of the former. Well, these questions are beyond my ability to unravel, although I am able to deduce from their lofty claims that these scientists are probably unfamiliar with Kant's powerful argument for the establishment of a notion of the self. There is a regrettable tendency for some scientists to believe that, as one of them recently put it, the conceptual problems of physics, at the cutting edge, are "too important to be left to philosophers." Given the novelty which they now, with some pride, ascribe to the view in their community that the observer may well be complicit in the experimentally determined reality of the quantum world, it would be no bad thing if they did open the pages of Kant's *Critique of Pure Reason*, where they would discover, I would hope with pleasure, that he, long before them, insisted that the world we take to be objectively real is created by the meeting of an unknowable *noumenal* world with the conceptualising and perceiving self, resulting in a *phenomenal* world which necessarily reflects both, and none of whose observed features can be considered to be entirely independent of the observer. How similar that is to the retreat from a totally objective reality which is currently under way! But leaving aside the mystery of consciousness, I do wonder where the idea of a universal virtual reality leaves the laws of physics as we know them. Are they too merely part of the programme; or do they hold sway, also, for whatever intelligent beings created it and set it running? If they do, then we *are* in the process of uncovering fundamental truths about reality per se, even if we can never know that we are. If they do not, then we cannot ever discover them, and cannot ever know that our laws are parochial. This is not a problem which those scientists can ignore – for to label our universe a virtual reality is, of course, to posit the existence of a parent universe which is not. I seem to remember that it was Socrates who most memorably insisted that there is wisdom in knowing that we do not know. But then I also recollect that I suspected his humility was a very sophisticated kind of arrogance: and I have the same feeling about the fun-loving mathematicians and scientists who postulate the existence of a world at the beck and call of a glorified play-station. They make, I think, the same mistake as the one which confounds all of the rather patronising word-games inflicted upon the academic world by structuralists: the failure to realise that, if you insist that everything that we believe to be the case is *really* an example of something else that is, always and everywhere, the case, then you lose the distinction between the two, and have failed to make an assertion with any meaning at all. And furthermore, you have left the status of everything that we believe to be the case unchanged, warts and all.....except that there is one exception, of seismic importance I should say, in the case of the notion of a universal virtual reality. In that gameworld, we go about our business as usual; but isn't there a paradox lying in wait for Descartes? *I think, therefore I do not exist.*

Whenever I visit Wales I bring with me a fragment of dark grey rock with part of a trilobite embedded in it. I often refer to it as part of my trilobite part, a name I gave it after reading that the vaguely convex part of a fossil – the bit that looks like the actual creature turned into stone – is called the part by professional fossil hunters, whereas the concave imprint which reveals itself after a stone is split is called the counterpart. My trilobite, which is headless but has its other two regions perfectly preserved, is, I feel fairly certain, a creature called *Ogygiocarella debuchi*, found in considerable numbers around Llandeilo and first described, though not named and indeed inaccurately described as a flatfish, by a Dr Lhewyd in an article, published in 1699, in the Philosophical Transactions of the Royal Society: *"Concerning some regularly figured stones lately found, and observations of ancient languages."* Dr Lhewyd was unwittingly prescient in his juxtaposition of stones and old words; his flatfish was subsequently named after Ogygia, a daughter of Amphion and Niobe familiar to those who have read the Aeneid, though they would have to have read it, I must admit, more carefully than I have. And the involvement of Wales in the rather undisciplined nomenclature of geology and paleontology was subsequently to burgeon: the Cambrian age, during whose early period trilobites first appeared, is of course named after the Roman word for Wales; and the Ordovician and Silurian systems, during which time they continued to flourish, are both derived from Celtic tribes that inhabited the Welsh borderlands. There is even an individual trilobite called *Merlinia*, associated with the ancient microcontinent of Avalonia. When I first learned of this, I found it hard not imagine that it was an enrolled trilobite, hidden in the great stone, which held and then released the sword which Arthur was alone able to pull out so as to set in train the story of the Round Table and the journey which would lead him finally to embark, with three queens, on his mysterious voyage to Avalon. When I looked at Gamallt this morning, I tried to imagine what it would have looked like if seen through the eyes of a trilobite. This was not, I told myself, as fanciful as it might seem; many mountains, after all, are ocean floors that have been heaved up into view, as anyone who has found fossil shells on high ground is forced to admit. Gamallt is such a mountain; the grey and green mudstone of which it is made was deposited, some 430 million years ago, in the shallow margins of a great marine basin which basked in the Silurian sun. The trilobites crawled on or swam above the sea floor, and could in a sense, therefore, have gazed at the very same stuff as I was looking at. There is a catch, however, with existential implications. Trilobites are the earliest animals in the fossil record with fully developed eyes: but these were no ordinary eyes. They were made of perfectly formed prisms: calcite crystals – calcium carbonate, the very substance of which the white cliffs of Dover are made. And the crystals were arranged in curved rows, like, for instance, the eyes of a dragonfly: particularly suited to the detection of movement. Compound eyes produce multiple images: so a trilobite able somehow to see the future of the floor over which it moved would presumably have seen not one Gamallt but hundreds or even thousands, arranged in tessellated ranks like the tents of a great army spread across a field of battle. My thoughts were presenting a Gamallt which I could not possibly engage with, even if I enlisted the help of metaphysical ruses or my fragmentary and slender understanding of science. And the problems that would have faced Dr Johnson if his skirmish with Berkeley had taken place in a post-Cambrian world dominated not just numerically by insects but by their way of seeing, hardly bear thinking about. I put my hand in my pocket and squeezed my trilobite fragment as if to render it sightless (someone once wrote, and I agree, that fossils are not dead – they are a life form) and reached into the other pocket for my sunglasses so as to bring a little further under control the tenuous link between my eyes and my mind. I was still affected by the Chablis which I had indulged in before stumbling into bed, and found myself entertaining extravagant suppositions about the involvement, not of Wales but of Gamallt, in the terminology of geological timescales. There were few rules, I reflected, governing the powerfully resonant words with which scientists calibrate and describe the momentous strata of life's early adventures. Devonian: named after a place where some English people live and some others take their holidays. Jurassic: the Jura mountains. Cretaceous: from *creta*, the Latin for chalk. Victorian scientists and adventurers bestowed these awesomely important words upon millions of years of evolutionary development on the basis of what they found, or where they found something: some specimen of life, or of rock, that fitted into a grander perspective. Why not Gamallt: Gamalltian – the place in Powys where some tweed-jacketed paleontologist had first discovered *a rock that had moved*. As for its age – I picked at words, like a musical novice tapping out alternative notes on a xylophone – words from the Latin list that starts with the Palaeocene and finishes with the Holocene: very seriously scientific but comically bound together in translation: *the ancient recent, the dawn of the recent, the little recent, the less recent, the more recent, the most recent, the wholly recent.* Gamallt, I reflected, is older than any of these; and yet I am a little tempted to appropriate the first and the last of them to bring it into the world as I now know it. We think of mountains as old, the more so, I think, if we are contemplating them during the later part of a day; but they disappear at nightfall and come back again the next day, as fresh and young as the morning. This simultaneous manifestation of the ancient recent and the wholly recent is perfectly captured by the painting which René Magritte completed in 1951 called *Souvenir of a Journey*. In a room stands a table; on it are a book, a bowl of fruit, an opened bottle of wine and a tumbler. All are made of stone; or rather they seem to have turned into stone. (Recently? or long ago?) As you scrutinise the picture you ask yourself: are these familiar items the fossilized remains of an ordinary domestic scene, preserved forever by a mysterious process of petrification? Or a visual representation of the way in which the memory of an occasion freezes it, like a snapshot which then stands in for the entire sequence of events of which it has become the defining moment? I prefer to think that they place before us the same assertion as that made, in positive and negative form, in Magritte's other paintings *The Human Condition* -where an easel placed in a window displays a painted landscape that is indistinguishable from what would be seen if the easel were removed - and *This is not a Pipe*, which warns us not to mistake what is painted for what is real. Was Magritte not insisting, as Milton did in Paradise Lost, that the mind is its own place? Magritte's table comforts me. Gamallt is as old as I want it to be. All I need now is to find a way to believe that it is where I want it to be also. To that end, I have pinned up onto the kitchen door the print which I brought with me of yet another of Magritte's works, which he painted in 1938 and gave the inexplicable name *The Domain of Arnhem*. It depicts a series of mountain peaks seen through a window, unremarkable save for the fact that one of the peaks is, unmistakably, the head of an eagle and those to each side of it resolve themselves into its wings. It is a mountain that could fly. Each time the door is opened, the painted image of mountains is replaced by Gamallt, a substitution which has not gone unnoticed by my companions in the longhouse. Isobel in particular has more than once asked me if I have considered obtaining a photograph of my mountain which, she has suggested, could be carried from our house each summer so that, on our return, I could consider my task accomplished, if only by proxy, with spectacular success. I suspect that there will be more suggestions of this kind before the holiday is over.

There is a fortuitously placed bed of stinging nettles at the edge of one of the fields which we cross on our descent to the river. It is, as far as I can ascertain with a reasonable degree of confidence, 519 yards from the base of Gamallt at its nearest point as we approach it from the longhouse. That distance – 475 metres, or if you like, 1,558 feet, which perhaps sounds more impressive – is equal to its height. I have placed a small, nondescript stone in front of the nettles to mark the spot and to signal to myself, each day, the moment when I can begin to get a feel for the magnitude of my ambitions. And completing the descent is, since I have no head for heights or indeed for holes in the ground, the only way I am likely to climb my mountain, although it involves crossing the river and the road so recently walked upon by the singing girls in order to be able to stand at its foot. I do not intend to move the stone, now that it has a purpose. Most decisions about emplacement have some validity, and I have always tried to allow the shape or provenance of the rocks which I gather to dictate in some way my own selection of position and attitude when I lay them to rest. I have placed an ammonite, which I found in the Swäbische Alb, at the foot of the Wisteria which, I think I mentioned in passing, I never prune. When deciding which face of the ammonite to display, I selected the one which gives the appearance of its growth having proceeded in an anti-clockwise direction. I say appearance because of course its other side gives the impression of clockwise growth. But there is a choice to be made; and mine was dictated by the fact that Wisteria sinensis, of which our specimen is an example, grows by twining its stems anti-clockwise; Wisteria floribunda, the other species usually offered alongside it in garden centres, twines them clockwise. It is as if some early plantsman had created two seedlings and set them, in pots, on either side of the equator so that they would mimic the behaviour of water, which, as gleeful demonstrators never tire of reminding us, spins either the one way or the other as it goes down a plughole depending on which side the container has been placed. All subsequent cuttings would then have followed suit, regardless of where they grew. It is only a fancy on my part; but the circular accretions of its growth seem so central to its identity that I leave our specimen untrimmed. Just so, I admit to myself from time to time, there are rocks which should be left undisturbed. And others which, however familiar their current resting place, should have been so left; for a rock can look out of place. There is such a stone, of granite, in the cobbled main street of Dent, which certainly looks as if it must have been brought to its present slightly incongruous resting place by dint of human labour. It is the site of a fountain – once the only source of water in Dent – and commemorates the reverend Adam Sedgwick, the Victorian geologist who investigated the landscape of North Wales and named the Cambrian system, and resided in the village during his early years, but played no part in the provision of the village water supply. I do not know whether there is a monument, in Wales, to Caradoc, the warrior who led the Silures in their fateful battles with the Romans and who is, therefore, by virtue of the role he played in securing the place of his tribe in history, the ultimate nomenclator of the 35 million year Silurian period which Sedgwick's colleague, Sir Roderick Murchison, is credited with recognising after scrutinising the rocks of South Wales. Perhaps the name of those who fought alongside him is enough. And the man of God from Dent and his aristocratic colleague did well enough, in that they used something of the past to name a remoter past, reversing, if only in words, Newton's arrow of time.

My doubts are creeping in again today. It has always seemed to me to be ironic that so many philosophers have rejected the ideas advanced by their predecessors, or their peers, by the identification of one or more *non-sequiturs* only to advance some rival claims which are themselves built upon a similar confusion of the logical connections between propositions. I have decided, this evening, that it is all the fault of Socrates. So many of his dialogues seem to reveal him as a pioneer of the stratagems that can be deployed in order to advance from one, innocently bland truth to a larger, supposedly inescapable conclusion by way of elementary stages of logical implication, when all along, one of his definitions – usually the first – is only one among many that might have been chosen. In my most gloomy moments, I fear that all philosophical arguments trundle along like that old teaser about the tortoise and the hare: they set off on a race, the tortoise having been granted a head-start, and, numberless bewildered students have long been told, by the time the hare has halved the gap between them, the tortoise has advanced a little, albeit not much; and when the hare halves the remaining gap, the tortoise has moved a little further; and so on ad infinitum. So the hare can never catch the tortoise. It is obviously, insanely wrong; as wrong when a hare has to do the overtaking as it was when it was first proposed, in around 464 BC by the Greek philosopher Zeno using Achilles as the chaser; but it is no easy matter to fault the logic of the steps that are taken to arrive at the conclusion, and no-one, indeed, has ever arrived at a simple and elegant refutation. Philosophers are either tortoises, like Immanuel Kant, a marathon man who plodded indefatigably toward a finishing line that perhaps only he could see; or hares, like Wittgenstein, who zig-zagged in the direction of one that he knew wasn't there at all. But like all philosophers, whether tortoises or hares, they thought that they were in the same race. And here I am wondering whose particular collection of non-sequiturs will help me enter into a causal relationship with a mountain. Unless I have committed one myself, in which case my project, too, has no finishing line. Then again, most philosophical theories end up by being defended in terms of a fallback position, a last-ditch simulacrum with none of the far-reaching implications of the original propositions. So I shall content myself for now with the depleted but powerful dogma that underpins the measurement of Zeno's racetrack: any bit of space, no matter how small, can, in principle, be subdivided. I'm not looking to move Gamallt very far, after all. And yet. So much has changed in the way we are allowed, by the keenest minds of our generation, or more to the point, the last few generations, to parcel up the world into units of knowledge. I doubt whether Zeno would have been able to propose his dilemma so confidently had he lived at the start of the twentieth century, and the less so if he had been acquainted with the limits to measurement set at that time by Max Planck. A modern Zeno would probably have been aware of the fact that, because light consists of waves a millionth of a metre long, no optical device can be used to measure, or indeed scrutinise, anything which is smaller than that. But the solution provided by the electron microscope is incomplete. The shorter the wavelength of whatever radiation is used to investigate ever finer detail, the more energy there is to assault the object under scrutiny; and at the *Planck length* the object collapses in on itself and vanishes. This length is, it seems, ten to the power of 19 times smaller than a proton. I don't know how small a proton is, and even the diameter of one of them would not amount to much of a lead for a tortoise, but it would be better than no measureable lead at all. And, according to those who understand such things, the time it takes for light to travel the Planck length – ten to the power of 43 times less than a second – is the shortest time interval that can ever be measured, so a stopwatch would be as little use as a tape measure if the hare really did come to the point of losing its lead. All this may seem a far cry from my project. But it tells me, I fear, that there is a limit to how modest my alteration to Gamallt's position can be – and it is already, I dare say, ridiculously insignificant to anyone not fully aware of my determination to clarify for myself once and for all the distinction between mind and matter. And what, indeed, would Berkeley have made of Einstein's response to that pioneering clarion call which successive generations of physicists have debated: *to be, in*

principle and not as a matter of experimental difficulty, not directly perceptible, is nevertheless to exist, even if only in the mind. ?
There are problems here; but I will steer clear of such unimaginable dimensions of space and time. When I first heard of them, protons seemed as tangible as marbles. That is enough to me; so one of them can serve to quantify my efforts. I will not concern myself at this point in time with how the measurement will be carried out. I cannot, as Isobel has pointed out, see Gamallt from our home in Cumbria; so any alteration in its position, even one that was, as she puts it, properly measurable, would not be evident to me by way of my senses. This does not trouble me, because I have been aware from the start that my alteration of the status quo is a matter for my mind and not my eyes. Her remark did, however, prompt me to reflect on the fact that *if* I were, by virtue of some miraculous enhancement of my visual acuity, to find myself able to resolve, from a high vantage point, the familiar shape of the mountain in the distance, I would at least be able to ascertain that it was exceedingly distant. We are of course given this ability, in no small measure, by the skill which we acquire in relating distance to the subtle changes of tone in the haze which we know accompanies the various degrees of remoteness – and landscape painters, those of Europe at any rate, made use of this when they produced the illusion of panoramas of the near and far-off by adding shades of green and blue to whatever was close to the horizon. The lunar astronauts were at a disadvantage in this respect, and in the absence of both air and dust, were quite unable to judge either the size or the proximity of even the more dramatic features of the pin-sharp terrain in which they wandered. They had to refrain from attempting to visit nearby hills which they knew, from information already supplied to them, were in fact gigantic mountain ranges vastly further away than they seemed to be; and one crew even abandoned an attempt to climb the rim of a crater when they were no more than a few dozen yards from it. I take comfort from this;

clearly the eye, so often said to be part of the mind, is only at its best when heat and dust conspire to offer, by way of the illusory colours which are so useful to artists, features which do not really belong to objects at all. So, then, when eventually I look at least in the direction of Gamallt, peering at what would be the vanishing point in a painting, it will be nearer because I trust it to be, and not because I can see that it is.

Our chairs are in a row, and we are all sitting, as we often do, watching Gamallt as it receives and absorbs the last moments of sunlight. Our backs are to the longhouse kitchen from which the aromas of tonight's meal are beginning to emanate. Each of us holds a glass of wine; whenever I see an empty one, I refill it from the bottle of Niersteiner Heiligenbaum which is underneath my chair. When it runs out I will replace it with the Niersteiner Hölle which is, for now, safely stashed away in the refrigerator. Another word game; it is possible to have many such pleasures with German wine. If you were feeling particularly devout, you could spend an entire week tasting the products of theologically named vineyards: on Monday, Graacher Himmelreich; on Tuesday, Kroever Paradies; on Wednesday, Johannisberger Hoelle; on Thursday, Wiltinger Gottesfuss; on Friday, Zeltinger Engelsberg; on Saturday, Oppenheimer Kreuz; and finally, on Sunday, a comparative tasting, perhaps, of Serriger Herrenberg and Briedeler Nonnengarten. These names come to mind because I sense a connection, in my tortuous route toward the finalisation of my collection of stones, between the search for ever-smaller components of matter and the infinite capacity for words to parcel-up the landscape of wine growing regions: a differentiation of the ground on the basis, ultimately, of taste. For a brief moment, I played with the thought of yet another variation on Berkeley's dictum: *to be perceived, is to be considered to exist separately.* It is a matter of regret, for me, that so many of the site names of Nierstein itself disappeared in the cold rationalisation brought into effect by the new vineyard register of 1971. No longer, except in the memories of ever more elderly local growers, is the red sandstone of Nierstein divided into such thought-provoking plots as *Uber der Rehbacher Steig, Ober der grossen Steig, Die 13 Morgen, Auf den 16 Morgen, Ober dem Hummertal, Hummertaler Höhl, Hinter den Häuser, Sommerbirnbaum, Kleiner Schmitt, Vorderer Rosenberg*. Only the words remain – just as, soon, only Thomas Mann's great novel *Der Zauberberg* will commemorate the Valbella clinic, soon to close, at Davos, the Alpine sanatorium which was its inspiration. Hans Castorp, the young hero of the novel, sat as we are doing each evening to contemplate the mountain which was to become part of his life for seven years. The power of words, and the power of a mountain: Mann himself wrote that he was urged to extend his brief visit to Davos by the resident physician, and, had he done so, might have been there for countless years: "If I had followed his advice, who knows, I might still be there! I wrote *The Magic Mountain* instead." In this way a real mountain brought about its own replication in the world of letters, and was ultimately responsible for the spiritual and perceptual enlightenment which were really Hans Castorp's reason for lingering near it for so long.

The bottle of Heiligenbaum emptied very quickly. We have moved on to the Hölle, and with it my attention has drifted to a recurring dream which I experienced last night, of another more brutal and pressing encounter with a mountain. Again and again, George Malory and Andrew Irvine disappeared into the snowy north col of Everest as they retraced, in grainy film images, their path toward the summit. I called out to them, but they seemed to set out repeatedly on their journey into history. When I woke up, I rid myself of the dream by reflecting on the gentler battle described by Mann, when Hans Castorp almost freezes to death in a snowstorm and is rescued from a potentially fatal doze by a dream of summer. But I would do well, I suppose, to remind myself from time to time that mountains are formidable opponents to all those who choose, no matter in what manner, to interrogate their power.

We have all been looking at the stars tonight, for their own sake and in the hope of seeing a display from the Perseids shower. I did not know, when I was a boy, that shooting stars are no more than tiny fragments of dust, or at most pebbles, left over as a residue each time a comet passes near the sun and is partly vaporised. I thought then that shooting stars fell to earth intact, just as I believed that rainbows touched the ground, and I often imagined that I would, one day, find one, still glowing and perhaps available as a lantern. My fantasy was not wholly inaccurate; because Comet Swift-Tuttle, the parent of the Perseid shower which was discovered in 1862, is scheduled to return and pass nearest to the sun in 2126, and, if it undergoes the significant fragmentation which it is known to have displayed in the past, may send a chunk of itself slamming into the earth on August 14th of that year. Now, as we all waited for the next moment of the less violent display taking place this evening, each of us hoping that we were looking at the right patch of sky, (some of us, I'm sure, hoping that *by* looking there, we would *make* a shooting star appear) I was reminded of an expedition I had undertaken as a boy during a week's camping on the Isle of Wight; an early evening search, with other boys, for female glow worms. We found at least a dozen waiting, like stars in the landscape, for wandering males in the long grass of a hillside, and put them all in a jam jar which we took back to our tent where we read comics by the mysterious greenish glow given off by our lantern. It seemed to me then that they shared a secret with the stars; a secret that was not manifested when the night departed and their unremarkable bodies were all that could be seen. The more solid they looked, the less remarkable they became. Many years later I was pleased to find that, according to Martin Rees, the astronomer royal, there are two billion photons for every atom that exists in the universe - a much less contentious claim than that made by the otherwise fairly sensible scientist Arthur Eddington, who stated in the Autumn of his career that he believed that he had accurately computed the exact number of protons and electrons in existence (two to the power of two hundred and fifty six, times one hundred and thirty six. Thus do scientists occasionally compensate for their lifelong commitment to the power of reason. I do not know of a similarly generous explanation for the much more frequently bizarre conclusions proffered by philosophers). Anyway, the preponderance of photons reassures me that one of my own beliefs – that light, as detected for instance by the Hubble telescope after travelling towards its mirror for as much as 13 billion years, is a much more permanent fixture, in the grand scheme of things, than matter – is a reasonable one. There is, lurking in the background, an uneasy suspicion, on my part, that any moderately competent physicist would correct me by pointing out that whatever might be true of clumps of matter, which can be agreed to be relative latecomers to the cosmic scene, the electrons and other bits and pieces that, suitably assembled, make up the primordial hydrogen and helium that have been present since a very short time after the big bang are actually quite a bit older than the majority of photons; at least those which embarked, however long ago, on their intergalactic journey toward the eye that we have put into space. Galaxies, after all, were some time in the making. But I choose to retreat, like the philosophers who salvage something from Zeno's paradox, to my own, surely sound and easily defended position: old light is a great deal more venerable than the oldest mountain; and whereas every mountain will one day succumb to the various forces which sculpt and erode it, all of the light which misses the Hubble mirror will, provided it does not encounter any other obstacle, continue to travel, time without end, unless it is, finally, unaltered save for a shift toward the red end of the spectrum, perceived somewhere unimaginably far away and transmuted by the operation of thought into matter at last – matter, I hasten to add, that will long ago have ceased to exist. I use this reasoning (however flawed it may be – and according to Brian Greene, it is suspect, for he writes in *The Elegant Universe* that light does not get old, and that we must follow Einstein's insistence that motion through space slows time, to the point where 'there is *no* passage of time at light speed') to further bolster my position with regard to Gamallt, with whom my own appointment is looming. Anything I can do to reduce its substantial occupancy of time and place will help me sleep soundly these last few nights. And it comforts and bemuses me to suppose that Berkeley was to receive, in a roundabout way, a vindication of his ideas by way of science. Armed with the discoveries of Edwin Hubble, he could easily have bolstered his theory of immaterialism, with its sly agenda of providing a conclusive proof for the existence of God, the ultimate voyeur, by way of a final, clinching definition: *to exist, or one day to exist, or to no longer exist, is to be perceived......*

That is not the end of the matter, though. Whenever I am by the river the ambiguity of that workaday philosophers' word, *perception*, presents itself to me. Do those travel-weary photons inspire knowledge of the dead and distant matter from which they departed, or something bound a little more closely to the mind? Ought we to say merely that we *believe* that they are messengers from a substantial past? I am not in fact troubled by this qualification, because the water always magnifies and re-enforces my tendency, shared by many people I suppose, to consider belief, at least when it suits me, to be the equal of knowledge. It is the life in the water that does this. The shallows at the edge of the river are teeming with small fish, some of them, like the minnows and loaches, as big as they will ever be; others, like fingerling trout, destined to grow into formidable adults; and big fish, like big stones, are more interesting than little ones. That must certainly have been true of the largest salmon ever to have been found in the Wye. Its weight was estimated at around 80 lb when it was discovered, dead, in May 1920: a fish that no-one had ever seen alive. And yet it was not an old fish; no salmon ever is, because they only live for about ten years. Along with one other fish – the Grayling – they have annual growth rings on their scales where the proof can be found; and even their few years have largely been spent at sea. They are no strangers to movement: some of them travel almost the entire one hundred and fifty miles of the river to spawn within four miles of its source below the slopes of Plynlimon mountain. Upstream and over gravel-bottomed shallows, over every obstacle of cascading water that stands in their way, it is movement against the odds. I take heart from that, as I do from the fact that a member of my family, a man who taught me to fish, was towed back and forth, in a heavy boat, for over an hour by a salmon which he had hooked not far from Tintern Abbey, many miles downstream from where I found my last holiday stone. It was only during the last few minutes, when the exhausted fish was finally raised to the surface, that he was able to see what had been pulling him around. And any fisherman will tell you that the most fecund parts of a river are the stretches of its water where fish cannot be seen: the dark, slow glides and eddies which are too deep to allow sunlight to penetrate very far. I remember ledgering for chub in the deep green frothy cauldron of Rushey Weir, on the Thames: a heavy lead weight took the bait far out of sight until it rolled along the riverbed, and the only sign of a bite was a sudden tug that bent the tip of the rod. In a deep river, to exist is to excite belief. Those who mock fishermen for sitting, supposedly without purpose, in order to stare all day long at water ought to reflect on the fact that so many people's beliefs are excited by what may not exist at all. I told myself this as I looked up at Gamallt and tried, very hard, to believe in the existence of particles of matter so small – 'a coagulation of the insubstantial', as Thomas Mann put it when he wrote *The Making of the Magic Mountain* in 1953 - that one of them could serve as the measure of my assault on its place in the landscape. But the moon appeared and rolled along the summit, and I was drawn into speculations concerning a question which it is quite beyond my ability to answer: is our satellite, now that it is lighter by the amount of rock removed by the Apollo crews, more inclined to drift away from the earth, or gripped in an even stronger gravitational embrace? Our meal had been a late one, and much of the wine I had consumed had been able to take effect before I ate. What with the extra wine with which we had celebrated the arrival of the Perseids, I was unable to remember how the mass of an orbiting body is a factor in its elliptical journey around its larger companion, and further confused when Plume invited me to consider the complicating factors of the abandoned hardware left on the moon's surface; Woody, the mass lost by our planet as a result of so many rockets achieving escape velocity; and Isobel, that gained by the arrival, over so many millennia, of significantly bulky meteorites. When we retired to the longhouse and sprawled, roughly in one of the broader halves of an ellipse, in front of the log fire which we always light to mark the ending of the day, I was too tired to give the subject any further deliberation.

After the food and the wine, dreams and uneasy speculations. The smoke from the fire had made my eyes begin to sting, forcing me to retire to our bedroom where I listened for a while to the rise and fall of the conversations and laughter which filtered through the splits and holes in the planks of ancient oak that formed the dividing wall. I did not fall asleep, nor did I stay awake. Something lingered, and it gradually took the form of fragments of the philosophical writings of Friedrich Nietzsche, assembled into a series of objections and refutations of the collection of ideas and speculations that had attached themselves to my project. *We operate with things that do not exist: bodies, divisible times and spaces....subtract interpretations, and there is no world left over....the apparent world is the only one....what we believe to be* *true is what happens to make it possible for us to live in a coherent way....truth is that sort of error without which a particular class of living creatures could not otherwise live....*I drifted into a sleep as shallow as the Silurian sea that once covered Wales, and collected trilobites which all turned out, when I offered them for identification, to be from the ten or so blind species which have been ascertained to have lived within its borders. I found another specimen and offered it to Zeno as a contender in yet another race; its name, I told him, was especially appropriate for his larger purpose: *Paradoxides paradoxissimus,* one so named because its significance was not understood by early paleontologists when they found it. Then I came face to face with Dr Johnson, who handed me a perfectly preserved example of *Opipeuter inconnivus* – named by Richard Fortey after he ascertained, from a friend, the Greek for "one who gazes without sleeping" – a trilobite that could see forwards, sideways, backwards, upwards (lenses pointing in all directions) – a species, Dr Johnson informed me, that kept the whole of the lower Palaeozoic in existence for Bishop Berkeley until it was fossilised, in its entirety, for those who subsequently announced its discovery. Toward the morning, I woke up convinced that Nietzsche had persuaded me to visit an art gallery, where he drew my attention to a painting, produced in 1510 by Pieter Breughel, depicting children playing marbles, and certain also that he had recited for me his uncompromising asseveration regarding the realisation of the self: *one should not wish things to be otherwise.*

I have given much – perhaps too much – thought to the selection of a precise location for what one of my companions has suggested I call my palpation of the mountain. He doubts a successful outcome; but I made my decision yesterday. There is a great slab of rock that juts out of the South side of Gamallt, close to a concavity just above the ground and easily within reach without undue effort. It is in almost perfect alignment for me; when I stand in front of it I am, if my map-reading is reasonably competent and my pocket compass is in order, facing our house in far-off Cumbria. When I was inspecting the pastel-shaded green and yellow lichens that covered much of its surface, I was tempted to push at it there and then, but instead I found myself following the movements of a small caterpillar which was looping its way across the rock. The classification of genera and species in the insect world is a little more sensible and consistent than the unruly system used by paleontologists; it is easy to see why the little traveller which I was scrutinising is a member of the *geometridae*, the group, all rather weak fliers, of which the November moth is an example. All of them, before they metamorphose into adults, move around by bringing the end of their stick-like body near to their head, a form of locomotion rendered necessary by virtue of the fact that their legs are confined to each extremity – nothing in the middle – and they have, therefore, to arch themselves along repeatedly, as if measuring the terrain over which they will one day fly. This struck me for a moment as resembling the most neurotically methodical advance planning, and I was overcome with fellow feelings of trepidation and then doubt, so I limited my resolve to the simple matter of requisition: it is this outcrop which will be my chosen point of contact with the rock. The matter was resolved, and I realised that there would be no going back. Success or failure now offer themselves for contemplation. Success will be an almost endlessly repeated moment – like Hokusai's *One Hundred Views of Mount Fuji*: a hundred ways of acquiring wisdom. Failure would be a miss for my arrow of time: a marble, rolled only once, that misses its aim. I dreamt last night that I was embarking on a pointless endeavour – throwing a proton against a mountain, as if cause and effect were a feature of reality which no variables, however extreme, could alter. My youthful appraisal of the claims of the infinitely clever world of physics reasserted itself. No scientific theory, I remember hearing, had ever been so successfully and repeatedly verified as quantum theory.

Matter, or what passes for it in the exquisitely small world of fundamental particles, does not obey predictable laws of cause and effect. Only probabilities reign: remote, as yet undiscovered deterministic variables are not waiting to be found. I was more impressed by the uncomfortable truth which quantum physicists complacently – it seemed to me – admitted and chose to push to one side: the comfortingly monotonous obedience of larger and more immediately tangible bundles of matter to the same laws as those flouted by the world of the quantum. From the marble to the galaxy, alterations in space and time have identifiable causes, not fuzzy probabilities demonstrable only by thought experiments. Here was the source of my worry: the proton, my measure of success or failure, belongs to the quantum realm. Gamallt belongs to Newton. Is my proton a conceptual Achilles, swift but unreliable, condemned to run a haphazard race against a slow but inexorably receding tortoise? Can you measure victory with something that never keeps still? Or push, even with a mountain as an intermediary, something that you cannot locate? I recall something I briefly mentioned a while back: Werner Heisenberg insisted, in 1927, that the position of a quantum particle can only be determined by renouncing the simultaneous measurement of its momentum. And Bach had earlier completed, in 1723, the preludes and fugues of his Well-Tempered Clavier in all 24 keys knowing that tuning any one of them rendered the others slightly untempered, so that only a compromise – an instrument so tuned that all notes were ever so slightly out of tune, but none harmfully so – would ever be possible in a single performance. Are we not, when we listen to that music, taken through the possibility of every act of measurement and calibration, of percussive sound and of the heart? Can we possibly believe, as the notes of the C major prelude unfold, that the clavier tuned to equal temperament has been rendered to even the tiniest and barely perceptible degree imperfect? I sense a chance here, a way out of my difficulties if I pay heed to Bach's example. *I lean on Gamallt; it shifts to the extent of the magnitude of one proton; unable to perceive what I have done, I nevertheless declare to myself that my mission is accomplished*, just as Bach ignored an unattainable goal in order to scale heights that only he could present to the world. Yet I am almost ashamed to compare the sleight of mind which could rescue me, in my little task, to the movements of thought by which he constructed his music. A quantum leap indeed. I will, though, not let go, without a struggle, my belief that even so small an achievement as the one I contemplate, is a work completed. John Donne, precisely a century before Bach in the winter of 1623, had written his own assessment of the relative importance of things large and small: *If a Clod be washed away by the sea, Europe is the lesse, as well as if a promontorie were...*

This morning, I have been scanning the South face of Gamallt with my telescope, searching for the man in a chequered shirt who climbs slowly up the precipitous-looking slope at roughly the same time each day. I think of him as Sisyphus, and I imagine him as carrying, perhaps concealed in the breast pocket of his shirt, a stone which he places at the summit, with the purpose of making it slightly but measurably higher, only for it to tumble down each evening and come to rest at the same spot from which he always, having picked it up yet again, commences his climb. My conjecture is fanciful, but not without an echo, albeit exceedingly faint, in the real world. In 1995, the film director Christopher Monger made a film, inspired by a tale recounted by his grandfather about a village in the Rhondda valley: *The man who went up a hill but came down a mountain*. It tells the story of a successful attempt, by Welsh admirers of a local hill, to rectify its failure, by a few feet, to qualify as a mountain. English ordnance survey officials, urged to check their disappointing result, are delayed by subterfuge until soil and rocks can be carried up the hill and piled on the top to bring it to the requisite height. The Sisyphus who appeared in my telescope each morning seemed, in my imagination, to be embarking on a similar task, and to be unaware that Gamallt's rejection of his offering, at the end of each day, lay in the fact that it is already, in my opinion, high enough. There is a peculiar authenticity, is there not, to the components of the world which we discover in the eyepiece of a telescope; it is as if we believe that something is more real if it can be magnified and still remain in focus, or, equally, if it can be distant and yet be drawn nearer so as to reveal details which we are pleased to believe were there before we saw them. And don't we feel that we are peering with unusual attentiveness, even though our eyes are being asked to perform no more sharply than they usually do? We often see things less, not more, clearly when the conditions demand particular effort on our part. And all astronomers know that it is easier to make out a faint object, such as a star of insignificant magnitude, by staring at it not directly but slightly to one side. Just so I strained my eyes, last night, to catch glimpses of the bats which visit our longhouse each evening. Many of them roost in the abandoned railway tunnel near the Victorian bridge which spans the valley of the River Marteg just before it feeds into the Wye, a hundred metres or so from the mountain. Their perception of Gamallt is of course not like ours; they build a picture of the world by mapping its reflection of the sounds they make as they fly. Is this – an interpretation of echoes – a secondary process, perception at one remove from reality? After all, it is not sounds emanating directly from things that are interpreted – it is the bats' own cries which bounce off them. The world is full of Cartesian bats: *I listen to myself, therefore I am.* It is ironic that these creatures, which make their way around with such velocity in the air, and those, such as barbel or catfish, which feel theirs with such delicacy in water, and which can therefore be said to exhibit extreme mastery of their environment, are arguably the most solipsistic individuals in existence, paying heed only to the nuances of what they hear or what they feel. I think that Berkeley, if he had been a bat, would have tried very hard to persuade his community that solid things, like mountains, never presenting themselves with the forcefulness of the retina but only with the pressure of the eardrum, are most definitely not real; and I imagine them all whispering their replies, countless times each second, so that entire symphonies of refutation reverberated around him: *thus, thus, thus, thus......*

Some of us have returned to the wetlands this evening so that we might witness the setting of the sun and the rising of the moon. We have assembled by the edge of a mysterious pool – I call it that because it is impossible to be sure, staring into its dark green water, that it is either enticingly deep, full of carp and tench and perhaps even a pike, or disappointingly shallow, offering no more than a temporary home to sticklebacks and water beetles. There is a thoughtfully situated table, with rough and ready seating, placed by an unknown lover of solitude at some time in the past who obviously considered, rightly, that its solidly hewn and rustic form would enable those who love to stare at water to do so, here, in comfort amongst the tussocks of grass and spike rush. Free of responsibility for tonight's meal, which is being prepared back at the longhouse, we brought with us a bottle of *Niersteiner Goldene Luft* so that we could drink a toast to whatever came by. As the sun sank down and faded, a few dragonflies flew their last sorties over the water, no longer hunting but preoccupied, it seemed, with marking out their territory a few more times before settling on the prominent stems of reed mace that lined the pool. These vertical landing strips have generally become known as bullrushes, as a result of a simple mistake by a Victorian painter. The true bullrush, *Scirpus lacustris,* has unobtrusive flower-heads and was given its rather muscular name in medieval times because of its size and vigour compared with other members of the family of rushes and their close relatives, the sedges. But when Sir Laurence Alma-Tadema took a break from painting scantily-clad young ladies in Greek or Roman settings to produce *Moses in the Bullrushes* in 1904, he used a specimen of *Typha latifolia*, known then, as now, at least to botanists, as reed mace; and so what many people call bullrushes owe their name to the enthusiasm of Victorians for the rather sentimental treatment of a biblical story. Perhaps it does not matter, because the error – compounded by the fact that it is the female flower-heads which we all find so conspicuous – has left us with a plant which is maybe a little more worthy of the name than the original.

We counted dragonflies for a while, but the bottle was soon empty; and Plume and I wandered around the pond in opposite directions so that we met at the far bank. When we looked at the water from our new vantage point, we could see the reflection of Gamallt, lit by the last rays of the sun; a perfect but inverted mirror image that looked for all the world as if the mountain had returned to the sea from which it had long ago sprung, but now inviolate, immune from the fretful caresses of its long departed progenitor. But then, as if by a pre-arranged signal causing them to arrive together, a small flock of swallows began swooping and twittering across the pool, dipping with miraculous precision to pick off the midges and gnats which loitered on the surface film. Each strike – better, by far, than any of those we had managed when skimming stones on the river – caused the surface of the water to ripple, and Gamallt began to tremble just as the moon threatened to replace the sun as the last light of the evening. I thought then of Newton's insights into gravity, of which, he wrote, after having demonstrated with mathematical precision its effects, that its *operation* in the presence or absence of immaterial particles that could convey its power was a mystery best left *"to the consideration of my readers"*; and of the momentous revolution ushered in by Albert Einstein, who invited the world to consider that this great force, far from manifesting its power through the medium of some still undiscovered wave or particle, is in fact transmitted, not instantaneously as Newton supposed but at that finite but awesome velocity which we casually refer to as the speed of light, and by distortions and ripples in the fabric of space-time itself. In this marvellous way did he put to rest the discomfort that Newton himself had revealed in a letter written in 1692: *"That one body may act upon another at a distance through a vacuum without the mediation of anything else, by and through which their action and force may be conveyed from one another, is to me so great an absurdity, that, I believe, no man who has in philosophic matters a competent faculty of thinking could ever fall into it."* The swallows were shifting the mountain by flexing the medium conveying the light by whose grace we gazed at it; but I preferred to think of them as offering a reminder of the curvature of inhabited space, which allows all journeys to be completed in good time even if not in straight lines. I said a few words to this effect to Plume, who made no reply but glanced, first, at the slowly disappearing form of Gamallt and then, with something approaching a smile, in the general direction of Cumbria; and then we simultaneously rejoined our wives by completing in reverse the two semicircular paths we had trodden around the pool. It was dark by the time we climbed up the path that led to the longhouse.

It rained last night. When we assembled for our daily walk to the river – one of the last we will be undertaking, as the end of our holiday draws near – it was clear that several inches must have fallen during the night, though we had all slept too soundly to hear it. The steep track that snakes its way down past a butterfly-filled meadow which had, after being mown yesterday, been patrolled by vigilant and hungry Red kites, was transformed by the passage of floodwater. An existing series of ruts and channels had been gouged and extended so as to create a long, gaping fissure, cleansed of mud and exposing the roots of the stunted hawthorn trees planted, long ago, to mark the course of the track along the edge of the meadow. This demonstration of the ability of water to sculpt what had seemed so solid induced a vague feeling of optimism in me as we approached the river.

There is such a testament to the erosive power of water at Malham Cove in Yorkshire, where those who arrive at the overlying limestone pavement have to negotiate the deep fissures carved by rain and sink water into the Carboniferous rock; though not far away, Malham Tarn bears witness to ageless durability, its water held at bay on a bedrock of unyielding Silurian slate. Erosion, too, is for the long term, of course; when you arrive at the foot of the great semicircle – over which, long ago, water poured at a greater height than Niagara Falls – the rock says to you *you are not going any further*. There are steps cut into the side; but the face of the Cove remains invincible to ordinary people. It is far from being a mountain, but the closer you get to its nearly vertical face the more it feels like one. Such a respectful response is not unreasonable for being commonplace; Pen y Ghent was long thought, by virtue of its impressive shape, to be the highest mountain in Yorkshire, and its height was reckoned, as late as 1770, to be 3,930 feet, when it is in fact 2,273 feet and outreached by five others. Those who peer at Everest are liable, though only in the most inconsequential way, to make a mistake in the opposite direction, at least if they leave their estimate of its height unchanged for a significant period of time; for its height is increasing by about one centimetre per year. It is also, as it happens, moving sideways, shifting a little northeast with the unequal colliding masses of the Asian and Indian tectonic plates whose buckling causes it to pile on the challenge which it presents to successive generations of climbers. If Gamallt was subject to the same kind of joyride, I would be without purpose.....

I was once urged to peer over the edge of the Cove, but retreated when my fear of heights took my pulse rate to an unsustainable level. When I sat down on the limestone to regain my composure, I caught sight of a pygmy shrew in one of the fissures from which stunted buckler ferns were growing, and pondered for a moment on the differences of measurement which prompt us to place things on the scale whose extremes we judge to be variations from what we call normal. The heart of a pygmy shrew beats around 1,000 times per minute, much faster than mine had when I approached the sheer fall that is my conception of the Cove face; but its frenetic expenditure of energy, which requires of it the consumption of food, such as woodlice, every 60 minutes, to the extent of its own bodyweight each day, leaves one thing remarkably unchanged. The number of times its heart beats, in its short life – always less than two years – is extraordinarily close to the total that is achieved by the average human heart. I have the feeling that numbers are involved, in ways that are both obvious and perhaps very obscure, in my sojourn here in the immediate hinterland of the Wye. I may have made calculations, totted things up, estimated my prospects of a successful venture into the unknown, too rashly. There is particular thought which threatens to dishearten me. I cannot stop myself from conjecturing that the man who I have been observing each morning may carry, along with the stone with which he burdens himself, a notebook in which he has written out, in order to stiffen his resolve, a number much noised about by physicists: a one followed by no less than 36 zeros. It is the extent to which the force of gravity – between, shall we say, two protons – is weaker than the electrical force which repels them from each other. The cumulative effect of gravity enables it to be a major player in the universe only because electrical forces, which can either repel or attract according to the charge of the particles involved, cancel each other out. Gravity never varies, so huge assemblies of particles enable it to begin to dominate. But if the man who ascends Gamallt so often takes heart from the example set by those minuscule components of the rock on which he scrambles, I surely may not. If a single proton can engage in such muscular pushing and pulling with its immediate companions – the other protons and the electrons and, for all I know (and I know very little of such things) the other bits and pieces of the quantum circus – then what am I thinking of, with my plan to take on even one as an opponent, singling it out as the token of success or failure when I see fit to shove it from where it has agreed to loiter, after jointly engaging with all its sidekicks in a mass negotiation with the force which binds the moon to the earth? What chance do I have, entering the ring with a positively charged proton and seeking to evade its capacity to attract me – I, who am, in the grand scheme of things undoubtedly, not to put too fine a point on it, a negative phenomenon? How can I possibly push it away? If, in the multiverse which I referred to earlier, there were a universe in which just two components had chanced to exist – me, a creature alive (though without purpose) made up of 10 to the power of 29 atoms (a number that has little meaning for me, except that I concede that it is ever so large) and – separated from me but co-existent – a single proton – then gravity would triumph as usual in the larger scheme of things, and we would eventually drift toward each other so as to fuse, momentarily, into a single entity; after which my old self would disappear, having entertained the last solution to Berkeley's protean equation: *I exist, therefore I am not perceived.*

For several minutes now I have been discussing with Isobel my uncertainty as to exactly when I should lean on the mountain. She suggests the early morning, just after sunrise, or else the early evening, just before sunset, for only at these times will my chosen slab be in the shade. I am inclined to favour a moment a little after midday, when it will be in full sun. I feel I will be at my strongest in sunlight; she, that Gamallt will be at its most receptive in the shade. Her recommendation worries me, in that I suspect that any movement which I can bring about at either of her chosen moments will be minimal, for my energy levels will be at their lowest, and possibly not amount to the tiny but measurable distance which I hope to achieve. But mine seems no better; I would surely be pushing on a rock already swollen with heat and whose Southerly face, therefore, would seem further away from Cumbria than it need be, certainly more than the modest length by which I will seek to push it closer. Her equanimity worries me most of all; I cannot really understand why she patiently debates with me what must seem, to everyone save me, the laughably unimportant details of a light-minded project. In the end, I let a simple matter of convenience sway me: it will be just after dinner. I had begun to feel a little ridiculous after she pointed out to me with just a hint of a smile that the expansion and contraction of the house would cancel out, to some extent, that of Gamallt. This was, she said, a key factor in her refusal to travel back to Cumbria so that she could, as I had envisaged, push against the far side of our house at the same time as I leant on the mountain, although I suspect that her unwillingness to forfeit a sizeable portion of the holiday played a role, too. And this was not the first time she had engaged in such gentle mockery; she had observed, after one of our exploratory excursions around the foot of the mountain, that I had been driven, by my selection of so large an addition to my collection, to clarify for myself the size of the smallest possible movement that could signal its appropriation. She even challenged me to formulate a 'scientific' declaration of the process whereby the distance decreased in inverse proportion to the size. I am not offended by these sallies. They tease me; but never once has she suggested that I am wasting my time. She has even suggested – I think it was one night recently when I kept her awake with endless recalculations of the direction and extent of the geosyncline which straddles the British Isles and which might, if my push on Gamallt were to correspond to the line of weakness which it reveals, add power to my elbow – that I must exercise caution. When I asked her what she meant, she switched on the table lamp at her side of the bed and showed me a postcard bearing a picture of the Lulworth Crumple, whose exposed cliffside strata bear witness to the immense forces which lifted and folded the limestone bedrock into something that is for all the world like an immense and untidy sign for a humpbacked bridge. I responded by raising an eyebrow, and fell asleep composing a reply to be delivered in the morning, to the effect that humans despite their weakness had shifted 300 million tons of stone to build the great wall of China. I forgot to mention it and later abandoned it as lacking even philosophical relevance to my own intentions. Lulworth has, in any case, always been associated for me not with anything as large and dramatic as an episode of stratified violence but with something altogether more gentle and diminutive: *Thymelicus acteon*, the Lulworth Skipper, one of the smallest British butterflies, first discovered there in 1832 and restricted now, as it was then, to a small stretch of the Dorset coast in the environs of the village. I ought to admit, by the way, that Isobel is not alone in this teasing, this friendly questioning of my project. Several of my companions have urged me – tongue in cheek, I feel certain - to consider a range of possible flaws in my project. Plume, for instance, chose to remind me of the internal debate among astronomers concerning the choice of a descriptive model for the expansion of the universe. Most cosmologists invite us to consider that it is simpler, somehow, to think of space itself expanding, pushing galaxies further and further apart, than to think of the galaxies themselves as hurtling away as if still reeling from the effects of the big bang. This supposedly more elegant explanation for the redshifted universe is limited, rather conveniently perhaps, in its application to the non-local space that lies between clusters of galaxies, as many galaxies within clusters do not appear to be separating. Some, in fact, are doing just the opposite; Andromeda, part of the modest little local group of which we are a member, is gravitationally bound to us with a force as irresistible as that between the earth and the moon, and is advancing toward us. Eventually, it will merge with the Milky way regardless of whatever other journey the pair of them are embarked upon. I try hard to see why space should expand so selectively, and I believe that the answer has something to do with gravity, which somehow allows space to expand without altering the relative position of objects that are intimately and forcefully stuck alongside each other, so to speak (and indeed it expands without pushing all the atoms in our bodies apart, since they too are bound by nuclear forces that are in any case far stronger than gravity). I have another motive for my doubts. I worried, for a while, to Plume's amusement, that my miniscule push on Gamallt would be cancelled out if it were already in the process of moving away from Cumbria, and I was all too aware that I do not have time to wait, as he recommended, for the start of the big crunch, as it is so inelegantly called, when a contraction of space would do the job for me. Things were further complicated when my attention was drawn to yet another of Newton's great ideas: the law of universal gravitation, whereby every object in the universe attracts every other object. How can you push away from you something you're attracted to? This niggling consideration of my gravitational friendship with Gamallt was one objection too many; I dismissed it in a decidedly unscientific manner, by telling myself that whereas Gamallt is of enormous significance to me, I mean nothing to Gamallt. I can allow myself the irrational luxury of thinking that its pull on me is a move in the right direction. My puny mass can be taken to lack any attractive force. Just so we assume that the earth orbits a stationary sun, whereas they each orbit what is I believe called their barycentre – their common centre of mass. Because the sun is so big, it is to all intents and purposes the stationary partner, subject to no more than tiny perturbation because the barycentre is located inside it. With the earth and the moon, the difference in mass is less dramatic; the earth's perturbation is more substantial. Were the moon a little larger, we might be forgiven if we came to the belief that they orbit each other. The opposite is true of me and Gamallt…

And again: yesterday afternoon, several of my companions offered advice, some of it sound, after I cut myself when replacing a rock which I had dislodged on the river bank. More provocatively, my friend Plume (I call him this because he writes under a pseudonym) - who has, throughout our current holiday, insisted that Gamallt is a hill and not a mountain - pointed to the beautiful purple flowerheads of Great Burnet which grew along the track back to the cottage and observed that its Latin name, *Sanguisorba officinalis,* and its reputed ability to staunch the flow of blood from wounds, came about as a result of the medieval *doctrine of signatures* whereby plants were believed to advertise their medicinal powers by outward signs, usually of colour or shape. He offered, I think a little mischievously, to accompany me to a second hand bookshop where we might, he said, find a tome which listed all such plants, with the possibility that there might turn out to be one which improved one's sense of proportion. I believe he may have indulged in this sally as a result of a conversation which we had early in the holiday concerning the definition of a mountain. He is of the view that the official position of the ordnance survey department is that a mountain has to be 2000 feet high and added, as if to underline his deference to official map-makers, that it must further, if it is located in Scotland, possess a distinct summit or peak. He went on, during our little discussion, to observe that it is the custom, in Scotland, on the part of climbers and walkers, to call mountains which just reach the minimum height Donalds; those between 2000 and 2500 feet, Grahams, those a little higher and up to 3000 feet, Corbets; and finally, those greater than 3000 feet, Monros. My opinion is that there is no formal criterion and that ordnance survey policy is to accept local nomenclature; in which case, I reserve the right to consider myself a local member of the community here, albeit an intermittent one; and as I see it, Gamallt is indeed a mountain; one, moreover, with a summit which I, given my fear of heights, regard as quite inaccessible. It is with that in mind that I have demurred from his suggestion that I call it Mohammed. I am a little uncomfortable with the presence, immediately South of Rhayader, of a hummock of land called Gwastedyn Hill, marked on Landranger 147 in the Ordnance Survey series as being some 2 metres higher than Gamallt; but I can live with discomfort, and I do not intend to engage any of the residents of the town in conversations about the monticules with which they are surrounded. And the next time we discuss the matter, I shall place before him a fact which I have only just remembered: that the famous and much discussed Ayer's Rock is well over a hundred metres less, in height, than my mountain, but nevertheless afforded because of its isolation the title of monolith – a label as grand, to my mind, as *Olympus Mons*, the 24 kilometre high volcano located in the northern hemisphere of Mars. Aren't words as substantial as the things they denote?

Today is our last full day; traces of the familiar melancholy which creeps up on me toward the end of our gatherings tell me that the time has come for me to bring my deliberations to an end. I know where to go, and my procrastinations have brought the matter of timing to a head, for the dinner which we are about to prepare, and enjoy in the shaded corner of the garden outside the longhouse, will be our last. My decision to act without concern for the sun or the shade but simply after the genial camaraderie of a midday meal, must be put into effect after this, our final assembly in the visible presence of Gamallt. I have not raised the subject with any of my companions; they are, in any case, maintaining what I am sure is a diplomatic silence. Probably, they all half expect to learn that the whole thing has been an intellectual game, shuffling logic and fantasy into inconsequential patterns that could have been straightened out by the application of a little common sense. But it is not so. I have to reach a conclusion. The morning began well enough, with mist gradually clearing to reveal a sunlit valley beyond the river. When, however, I trained my telescope on the slope for a final glimpse of the man who toiled up it, the eyepiece already focused from yesterday's session, he was nowhere to be seen. I used several magnifications to carry out a thorough search; all to no avail. He was not there as a speck in the distance, nor, therefore, did he loom large in my field of view. His absence was a cue for me to make up my mind, although the alacrity with which he had seemed to set off on each of his ascents prompted me to see myself as a competitor in another race conceived by Zeno, but rendered futile in that I would be set the task of catching up with him despite being a ponderous and doubt-ridden tortoise. Fortunately the meal, punctuated as it was by moments of boisterous humour, has cleared my mind and enabled me to prepare myself for the task in hand. There were some last-minute negotiations which fortified me despite the fact that I was, almost certainly, being humoured for the sake of what was probably thought of as my peace of mind. Woody offered to observe me through my telescope to ensure, as he put it, my continued presence at my chosen point of contact with Gamallt. Plume's wife agreed to leave immediately so as to arrive at the bilberry–strewn slope before I did, where she promised to gather and eat as many berries as possible so as to lighten, if only by a few handfuls, the load awaiting me. Plume himself informed me that he proposed to remain behind and, by consulting one or two of the many books in his possession, endeavour to work out where, and at exactly what time of day, Dr Johnson had issued his refutation of Berkeley's thesis about existence and perception, with a view to making an informed guess as to the type, and precise age, of the stone which played so vital a role in the episode. I found some considerable satisfaction in having provided, I suppose I should say unwittingly, a forum for these mirthful interventions. And so it was that the moment arrived for me to set off, with Isobel by my side, for the clump of nettles that would signal the countdown to my arrival at what I have begun to think of as my second home. More than once, as we walked over the Victorian bridge that would give us access to the path leading to the concave indentation in the rock face, I found myself glancing over my shoulder, half expecting to glimpse the ghostly form of a second and more substantial mountain behind me. It was Plato's parable of the cave that was haunting me. We are, he said, like prisoners chained to the floor in a cave, unable to turn our heads and so not able to see the fire that, burning behind us, casts ghostly and flickering shadows on a wall deeper into the heart of the cave; shadows, perhaps shadows of ourselves, which we mistake for reality. In his discourse, Plato indicates what further mistakes must be overcome if such prisoners, upon their release into the world outside the cave, are to arrive at a final enlightenment as to the nature of that which is ultimately real; but it is the preliminary image of enchainment which has captured the imagination of generations of curious readers, suggesting as it does that what we perceive is not at all as real as we take it, so confidently, to be. I supposed, as we neared the rock face, that the two lives I have lived – of the mind and of the body – reflected two very different ways of responding to Plato's evaluation of the senses. On the one hand I have pursued, in my own modest way, the ideas he cultivated, or at least the dialogues and disputes which his proposals generated, leading me to discover some sympathy for the scepticisms and unworldly passions of philosophy. But I have for a long time also nurtured a taste for the untroubled approach to life in a cave suggested by the wall paintings at Lascaux: people undeceived by the fires they surely lit, and using the light of candles or torches to depict for themselves the real inhabitants of a world outside; creatures with which they had long been familiar and whose own capacity for ghostliness could be itself confined to images in darkness, leaving them free to roam, when they chose, in the light of the sun.

After we reached the slab I positioned myself so as to be able to lean on it with as much of my weight as possible. With the palm of my hand resting against its vertical face I splayed out my fingers and made ready to press down on the surface, flexing my hand so as to cup it against the right angle formed by the edge of the rock. I dislodged a sliver of lichen-free material from a small circular pit on the surface; the exposed hollow was damp and immediately disgorged a woodlouse, which I recognised as *Armadillididium vulgare*, the pill woodlouse, so-called because of the ability it shares with the armadillo to roll itself into a protective ball. For a split second its refuge reminded me of the 'choc holes' which I had made as a child and which were the target resting places of the marbles with which my generation had played competitive games. The woodlouse crawled away from its uncovered niche and, after a few stops and starts, found another crevice into which it could disappear, as if anxious not to be seen. As I watched it I found myself envious of its intimate relationship with Gamallt. Everything about the creature was like an equation whose solution was to be found amongst the scree; but it had merely to live in order to confirm each equation. Its resemblance to a trilobite was fortuitous – they are not closely related – but when one creature looks so like another it is hard not to make a connection even where one does not exist. My inability to rid myself of the idea that fossilised trilobites were to be found embedded somewhere in the strata of Gamallt added to the inclination, which now took hold of me, to magnify the track of the little isopod into a great avenue of meaning stretching back, and forth, in time. I recalled, in the story by Hermann Hesse, Siddhartha's words to his old friend Govinda: his affirmation of love for a stone *because it has already long been everything and always is everything.* It was at this moment that doubt loomed large in my mind, and I wondered if my desire to shift Gamallt, even by so microscopic a distance, might be the hopelessly wrong answer to an equation which should begin with the very thing which I thought was its solution. What if it was Gamallt that was bringing about a change in me? I reached out and took hold of the woodlouse before it could disappear, and dropped it on the palm of my right hand so that I could scrutinise it. Then I placed my other hand back on the slab and leaned on it. At precisely that moment I admitted to myself the most glaring – and I suppose to everyone else the most ludicrously obvious – flaw in my fastidious plan. How was I really going to know if the mountain had moved?

I stared at the woodlouse. It had ceased to move and had rolled itself up into a ball. It looked smaller; and at that moment I became aware of the futility of my struggle with the mountain. All I had to do, to alter it, was to cease trying to. Then it would relocate itself.

The ground had shifted. All of the modifications which I had gratefully seized upon amounted to a long line – one of many, but one I had preferred – in the history of thought from Democritus and Leucippus, who first postulated a reality made up of indivisible and indestructible atoms inhabiting a void and offering the possibility of perceptual knowledge only of things that consisted of them, not of the atoms themselves – through the momentous achievements of Isaac Newton, whose primitive particles were *"so very hard, as never to wear or break in pieces"*, and on to what used to be called modern physics, in whose scaffolding there was, for a while, a stubbornly surviving notion of minuscule items of reality behaving for all the world like microscopic solar systems. But after Rutherford used the tiny ammunition that emanated from radioactive substances to bombard and explore the structure of the atom, and discovered that the space between the nucleus and its orbiting electrons was vast – the assembled protons and neutrons of the nucleus akin to a pinhead in the dome of St Paul's, the electrons even smaller and somewhere near the periphery – all ideas about the solidity of things began to falter. They even led the painter Kandinsky, if one of his stories is to be believed, to renounce as futile the depiction of the physical world. And they seem to face abandonment now that quantum physics has ditched the idea of particles as fundamental items of reality; for one thing, particles, it seems, must also be thought of as waves; and changes in what one might modestly call their circumstances may not be brought about by identifiable causes but by the operation of a rather mysterious manifestation of probabilities. Thus we are told – and there doesn't seem to be any arguing with it – if a radioactive substance has a half life of a thousand years, then after that period of time approximately half its atoms will have decayed. But there is no point whatsoever in asking what property was possessed by the departed atoms, causing them, rather than those they leave behind, to take their leave. There is, we are told, no such property to be found. Probability alone sees to it that they are gone. Likewise, the great physicist Richard Feynman has insisted that we have to accept that four percent of the photons that strike a sheet of glass will be reflected and ninety six percent of them will penetrate it. And we do not know why. As he points out in *The Strange Theory of Light and Matter*, "....that's the way it is. Nature permits us to calculate only probabilities." I will limit myself to saying that this remarkable truth seems to show that explanations, in physics, now include the idea that fundamental descriptions of what I stubbornly continue to think of as reality now embrace the idea that nature, even if statistically predictable, is, in part, unknowable. And the smallest components of reality are not simply infinitesimally small versions of what we know as objects but are rather defined in terms of energy, obeying few or none of the laws formulated by Newton or even those lingering in the world-picture of early nuclear physics. Their transmutations do not seem to take place in a way that can be described as movement through space and time, but rather as a succession of vibrations which cause them to manifest themselves as this or that item of what may finally be called *what there really is*. This is closer to Heraclitus –"*All things move, and nothing remains still*"- and the Eastern mystics, and reminds me also of the spiritual principle behind the patterns of Islamic latticework: that what is solid is simply congealed spirit. And this idea gives me confidence, also, to put behind me my lifelong assumption that what is truly real is incontrovertibly solid, which I have clung to alongside its bedfellow: that nothing can be more fundamental than the terminally small. The mind has no terminus. Why search for something impossibly small, in order to shift the mountain whose counterpart was imprinted within me the moment I first glimpsed it?

Now, as I stand with one hand pressed against the slab and the other clutching the woodlouse, I see that my preoccupation with the choice of the sun-drenched or shaded mountain was irrelevant. I have only to look at it. Sunlit, it reveals itself to me as unshaded; in shadow, it announces itself as unilluminated. There is no need to search for a Gamallt that is somehow more fundamental, neither yin nor yang. It is what I choose to perceive it to be. It is neither large nor small, but something that defies measurement. Sequence, process, change. Gamallt does not need to be moved, nor approached at this or any other time, because its suchness is not fixed. As I release the enrolled woodlouse to trundle, having become a marble, down the slope, I see that the hugeness and immobility of this great rock are dependent upon everything – its interrelatedness with every one of the objects with which I have been concerned, including the marble long ago tossed into the stream when I was a boy. Watching the woodlouse disappear into the multiplicity of the scree, I relinquish my hold on the jutting slab: the proton, the marble and the mountain are one; and they are nothing. I walk back to the voices of those with whom I came to this place, mingling with the sounds of the river, and rejoin the flux from which I had thought to differentiate myself. I had laboured under the aegis of the classical definition of measurement: "the correlation of numbers with entities that are not numbers". But did not Pythagoras say that everything is a number? I walk on with Gamallt now behind me, older than it has ever been, listening as it whispers to me Buddha's last words: *Decay is inherent in all compounded things. Strive on with diligence.*

It seemed that Heraclitus and Berkeley had won after all. But after we had packed the car and said our goodbyes, I put on my walking shoes. And when we completed the circle that led us from the house and across the river and on to the road that pointed home, I stopped when we drew level with Gamallt, the great rock that had begun to feel like a second home. I got out of the car and walked over to a part of the great rock face that was dappled with shadows cast by a clump of Mountain Everlasting, *Antennaria dioica*, so called, in English, because it springs up every year on the same spot and, by botanists, because it is always either male or female, never self-fertile, hence, in Greek, *dioica* or two houses. I gazed at the rock, reflecting on Kant's words as he foretold the science that was to come: "Up to now it has been assumed that all our cognition must conform to the objects; but let us once try whether we do not get farther with the problems of metaphysics by assuming that the objects must conform to our cognition." I recalled, as well, his great and very human words of advice to (I like to think) both philosophy and science: "If one cannot prove that a thing is, he may try to prove that it is not. And if he succeeds in doing neither, as often occurs, he may still ask whether it is in his interest to accept one or the other...hypothetically." Then I gave Gamallt a kick: just in case. A flurry of movement caught my eye; from a network of cracks near the mark left by my shoe, a stream of woodlice poured forth like animated marbles. But they found other hiding places, and disappeared before I had time to count them, or watch them as they turned back into trilobites.

----------- O -----------

Made in the USA
Charleston, SC
26 October 2014